By Bart Coughlin
Illustrated by Leticia Lacy

T#: 623990

rhcbooks.com

ISBN 978-1-9848-3056-2

Printed in the United States of America

10 9 8 7 6 5 4 3 2 1

nickelodeon

LUCKY

The Adventures of the
Unluckiest Leprechaun

Random House 🏠 New York

Once upon a time, there lived an unlucky leprechaun named Hap. Many years before, Hap's great-great-grandfather Jedidiah McSweeney's pot of gold had been stolen by a giant dragon. From that time on, the McSweeney curse was passed from generation to generation—until it splatted right onto Hap McSweeney's head.

Hap's father, Pappy, often said, "It's not BAD luck. It's McSWEENEY luck." Hap couldn't tell the difference.

But even though Hap's life seemed like one misstep after another, he knew that every dark cloud had a silver lining. In fact, Hap had *three* silver linings: his best friends! They were Shannon, the adventure-seeking elf; Sammy, the gentle giant of a troll; and Reggie, the hyperactive gremlin.

One day, Hap and his friends went on a class trip to Houlihan Tower. Mr. Houlihan was rich and very, very lucky.

Miss Doris, their fairy godteacher, told them to be on their best behavior.

Unfortunately, Hap's bad luck was never far away. Just as the tour started, Hap fell into a janitor's bucket and bounced down some stairs. He crashed into a security room filled with video monitors.

EMPLOYEE ONLY

CAUTION WET FLOOR

Hap couldn't believe what he saw
up on the screens. There, in a treasure
room, was his family's lucky pot of gold!

Back at school, Hap told his friends what he'd seen. He knew he could lift the McSweeney curse—if he could just get the gold back.

The friends formed a plan. During their field trip, Mr. Houlihan had told the students he was hosting a big gala that night. It was the perfect cover for them to sneak in and get the pot of gold!

"Houlihan Tower will have tight security," Shannon said, sculpting a mini version of the tower with some food. "But you know what won't?" She stuck a sprig of asparagus near the mashed-potato tower. "One Beanstalk Place, right across the street. All we have to do is zip-line from One Beanstalk Place to Houlihan Tower!"

That night, outside the tower, Hap realized that the plan would be a lot harder than it sounded! Sammy was nervous, too.

"Anybody else having second thoughts?" asked Sammy.

"Nuh-uh," said Shannon. "This is going to be awesome!" The fearless elf tied a rope to an arrow and fired it over to Houlihan Tower. *Thunk!* The arrow stuck in the side of the concrete building.

"Wheeee!" Shannon zipped across the rope. Reggie quickly followed her.

Hap and Sammy took off together—and got stuck halfway across!

Hap slipped from Sammy's back and accidentally pulled down his pants! "Definitely don't look down now!" he shouted to Sammy.

Just then, the rope snapped! The friends held on and crashed into the side of the tower.

Hap and Sammy crawled up to a balcony to join their friends. Shannon unlocked the door and the team crept inside.

"What about disguises?" Hap asked.

Reggie had something better: Miss Doris's fairy dust! The mischievous gremlin threw a handful of the dust into the air. Suddenly, Sammy was dressed as a waiter and Reggie as a handyman. Hap and Shannon looked like gala guests in their fancy clothes.

The team members put tiny devices in their
ears so they could communicate with one another.
Then they split up and went to work.

Reggie made it to the security room, where he
found a blueprint of the tower. "There's a secret
passage to the treasure room behind the big
painting of Houlihan!" he said.

Hap gulped. To get to the big painting, he had to dance across the ballroom. "I'm a disaster normally, but dancing? That's a catastrophe!"

With Reggie's guidance and Shannon as a partner, they made it across the floor to the portrait.

"Thanks, Shannon," said Hap. "You're better than a four-leaf clover!"

Hap and his friends slowly snuck through the secret door. On the other side was a giant cavern. At the center, perched high on a tower of rocks and surrounded by a lava moat, was the McSweeney pot of gold!

Hap couldn't believe it. He was finally going to get his family's gold back and lift the curse! It was all he'd ever wanted.

Suddenly, a figure stepped out of the shadows.
It was Mr. Houlihan!

"I have a lovely story to tell you," he hissed. "It was
a full-moon night. A fool of a leprechaun—pot of
gold in hand—was walking through the forest when
a huge dragon appeared." He laughed. "Your great-
great-grandpappy looked so frightened. That was
when I swooped down and grabbed the pot of gold
out of his hands!"

The villain cackled as he opened his mouth to reveal a long forked tongue. Instantly, horns grew from his head and wings unfurled on his back.

Houlihan wasn't a man at all! He was a DRAGON—the same dragon that had stolen the McSweeney gold!

But Houlihan's luck was about to run out. Hap ran as fast as he could while his friends bravely fended off the dragon.

Hap clambered up the tower's steep stone steps. At the top, the McSweeney pot of gold glistened before him. He put his hands on it—and felt a surge of luck rush through him. "I . . . feel . . . LUCKY!" Hap cried.

That feeling quickly disappeared when he saw that his friends were in trouble. The dragon had wrapped them up in his tail and was dangling them over the lava moat!

"It's your decision, McSweeney!" growled the dragon. "Choose the gold or your friends, you luckless loser."

Hap clung to the pot of gold. "Maybe I am a luckless loser," he told the evil dragon, "but you know what? My luck has brought me the three best friends I could ever hope for." He carried the pot to the edge of the drop-off. "It appears you need this gold a lot more than I do. You want the gold? Then go get it!"

With a great shove, Hap
tipped the pot of gold into
the lava. The greedy dragon
chased after it, but the
treasure was gone.

Now, just like the McSweeneys,
the dragon had lost the pot of gold
and was cursed with bad luck.
   A cloud gathered over his head.
   Rain fell on his snout.
   Bolts of lightning stung his tail
as he flew away.

"I can't believe you gave up your family's gold for us, Hap," said Sammy.

"You'll be cursed with bad luck forever," Shannon said sadly.

Hap smiled. He had his friends, and that was all he needed. Besides, it wasn't bad luck. It was McSWEENEY luck!

Hap's life returned to normal. Well, as normal as the life of an unlucky leprechaun could be. But he still had his friends.

And that made him the luckiest leprechaun in the world.